Peach AND Plum

Rule at School!

For my Ridgeview Elementary teachers,
who taught me well.

About This Book
This book was edited by Andrea Colvin and designed by Carolyn Bull.
The production was supervised by Bernadette Flinn,
and the production editor was Marisa Finkelstein.

Little, Brown and Company
Hachette Book Group
1290 Avenue of the Americas, New York, NY 10104
Visit us at LBYR.com

First Edition: February 2023

Little, Brown and Company is a division of Hachette Book Group, Inc.
The Little, Brown name and logo are trademarks of Hachette Book Group, Inc.

The publisher is not responsible for websites (or their content)
that are not owned by the publisher.

Library of Congress Cataloging-in-Publication Data
Names: McCanna, Tim, author, illustrator.
Title: Peach and Plum : rule at school! / Tim McCanna.
Description: New York : Little, Brown and Company, 2023. | Series: Peach and Plum ; 2
Audience: Ages 6–9. | Summary: "Peach and Plum get separated by a new substitute teacher
with new rules" —Provided by publisher.
Identifiers: LCCN 2022019866 | ISBN 9780316306300 (hardcover) | ISBN 9780316306409
(trade paperback) | ISBN 9780316347358 (ebook)
Subjects: CYAC: Graphic novels. | Stories in rhyme. | Peach—Fiction. | Plum—Fiction.
Schools—Fiction. | Teachers—Fiction. | LCGFT: Graphic novels.
Classification: LCC PZ7.7.M41264 Pk 2022 | DDC 741.5/973—dc23/eng/20220525
LC record available at https://lccn.loc.gov/2022019866
ISBNs: 978-0-316-306300-0 (hardcover), 978-0-316-30640-9 (paperback),
978-0-316-34735-8 (ebook), 978-0-316-34756-3 (ebook), 978-0-316-34772-3 (ebook)

PRINTED IN CHINA

APS

Hardcover: 10 9 8 7 6 5 4 3 2 1
Paperback: 10 9 8 7 6 5 4 3 2 1

Peach AND Plum

Rule at School!

Tim McCanna

LITTLE, BROWN AND COMPANY
New York Boston

I'm Peach!

I'm Plum!

And that's our **school.**

FRUITDALE ELEMENTARY

SLOW

CROSSING GUARD

What's up, Ms. Prune?

STOP

She's super **cool.**

5

CONTENTS

Is this the end for Peach and **Plum?**

I brought
my parrots...

CHAPTER 2
Lost Charm

She had a swirly rainbow **horn.**

Some baseball cards.

A robot **arm.**

One glove.

Two pens.

Three keys.

My charm!

41

46

Persimmon?

Kiwi?

Apricot?

Could they be members?

I think **NOT.**

They're gone.

That's good.

No muss.

No fuss.

The party's over.

WHAT?!

NO WAY!

It's time to leave.

I want to **stay**.

Humph.

Happy birthday, Honeydew!

THE END

One day, as Chicken Little walked...

...an acorn hit him...

He met a turkey...

...goose...

...and duck.

Then told them of their awful **luck.**

Backstage...

Where's Plum?

I'm feeling **sick.**

Then Foxy Loxy said with **glee...**

I know a shortcut. Follow **me!**

But now we better move our **feet.**

They're lining up on Second **Street...**

The walkathon is **underway!**

Each lap supports our school!